Adventures of the
laziest cat

by

Injamul Alam

Boibili

Contents

...

The Lazy Life of Oscar

1

Oscar was a street cat who lived in Istanbul, Turkey. He was known throughout the neighborhood as the laziest cat around. He spent most of his days lounging in the sun and begging for food from the kind-hearted locals.

One day, Oscar was basking in the warm sunshine when he heard a commotion down the street. He lazily lifted his head to see what was going on and was surprised to see a beautiful white cat being carried by a young woman. The cat's name was Sassy, and she was traveling with her owner on a trip through Europe.

Oscar's heart skipped a beat when he saw Sassy. She was the most beautiful cat he had ever laid eyes on, with bright green eyes and a fluffy white coat. He knew right away that he had to meet her.

But Oscar wasn't exactly the most adventurous cat around. In fact, he was quite content to stay in his cozy spot in the sun all day. So he tried to think of a creative way to meet Sassy without having to put in too much effort.

Finally, he had an idea. He would wait until Sassy's owner left her alone for a moment, and then he would waltz right up to her and strike up a conversation. It was a foolproof plan.

Or so he thought. As it turned out, Sassy was not the kind of cat who took kindly to strangers. When Oscar approached her, she let out a loud hiss and swatted at him with her paw.

Oscar was taken aback by Sassy's reaction, but he was not deterred. He had never met a cat he couldn't win over with his charming personality. So he decided to try again, this time with a little more caution.

He sidled up to Sassy and began to purr softly. "Hi there, beautiful," he said. "I couldn't help but notice you when you walked by. My name is Oscar. What's yours?"

Sassy rolled her eyes and let out an annoyed sigh. "My name is Sassy, and I'm not interested in making small talk with a lazy street cat like you," she said.

Oscar was taken aback by Sassy's harsh words, but he refused to give up. He knew he had to find a way to get through to her.

"Come on, Sassy," he said. "I know I'm not the most energetic cat around, but I have a lot of love to give. And I think you're the most beautiful cat I've ever met. I just want to get to know you better."

Sassy looked at Oscar with a mixture of frustration and amusement. She had to admit, there was something endearing about his persistence. And deep down, she couldn't help but feel a little drawn to him.

Despite her reservations, she found herself softening towards Oscar. And as they continued to talk, she began to see that there was more to him than just laziness.

In the end, it was Oscar's charming personality and his relentless pursuit of Sassy's heart that won her over. And as they sat together in the sun, they knew that they had found something special in each other.

The rest, as they say, is history. But as for Oscar, he knew that he would always be remembered as the laziest cat who ever fell in love.

...

2

Oscar and Sassy's romance was off to a rocky start, but as the days passed, they found themselves growing closer and closer. They spent their days lounging in the sun and exploring the city together, and Oscar couldn't believe how lucky he was to have found such a wonderful companion.

But alas, all good things must come to an end. Sassy's owner had decided it was time to continue their journey and move on to the next city. Oscar was devastated when he heard the news. He couldn't bear the thought of being separated from Sassy.

"But Sassy, what about us?" Oscar asked as they sat together on a park bench. "I can't imagine my life without you. Can't you stay a little longer?"

Sassy looked at Oscar with a sad expression. "I wish I could, Oscar," she said. "But my owner has plans for us. We have to go."

Oscar's heart sank at the thought of being apart from Sassy. He knew he had to come up with a plan to keep her by his side.

"Well, then I'll just have to come with you," he said. "I'll be your traveling companion. We can see the world together."

Sassy laughed at the idea. "Oscar, you're a street cat," she said. "You can't just up and leave everything behind. It's not that simple."

Oscar knew she was right, but he couldn't bear the thought of being left behind. He had to find a way to make it work.

"Fine, then I'll just have to find a way to follow you," he said. "I'll come up with a plan, I promise. You'll see."

And with that, Oscar set out to come up with a way to stay by Sassy's side. He knew it wouldn't be easy, but he was determined to make it happen. He was in love, and he would stop at nothing to be with the cat of his dreams.

...

3

Oscar was heartbroken when Sassy left Istanbul, but he refused to give up on their relationship. He spent the next few days trying to come up with a plan to follow her and be by her side.

He knew it wouldn't be easy, but he was determined to make it happen. He scoured the internet for ideas and even asked his feline friends for suggestions.

Finally, he came up with a plan. He would hitch a ride on a cargo ship heading to Florida, where Sassy was headed. It was risky, but it was the only way he could think of to be with the cat he loved.

Oscar knew he had to act fast, so he set out to gather the supplies he would need for his journey. He packed a small bag with a few necessities and set off to find a ship heading to Central Europe.

As he wandered the docks, he was approached by a gruff-looking sailor who asked what he was doing there. Oscar hesitated for a moment, not sure if he should trust the stranger. But he knew he had to take a chance.

"I'm trying to get to Florida," Oscar said. "I'm in love with a cat who lives there, and I need to find a way to be with her. Do you know of any ships heading that way?"

The sailor chuckled and ruffled Oscar's fur. "Well, I'll be darned," he said. "I've never met a cat with such determination. Come with me, and I'll see what I can do."

Oscar's heart raced as he followed the sailor to a small cargo ship. He knew this was his chance to be with Sassy, and he was willing to do whatever it took to make it happen.

As he boarded the ship and settled into his makeshift cabin, Oscar couldn't help but feel a sense of excitement. The sailor explained the possible roads and challenges to Oscar. He knew this would be a journey filled with adventure, and he couldn't wait to see what lay ahead.

...

4

Oscar's journey across Europe was not without its challenges. As he traveled from city to city, he faced all sorts of obstacles and encountered a wide range of characters.

One of the most memorable stops on his journey was in Hungary, where he met a kind-hearted man named Oliver. Oliver lived in a cozy little cottage on the outskirts of Eger and took Oscar in as a pet.

At first, Oscar was thrilled to have a warm place to stay and all the food he could eat. But as the days passed, he couldn't shake the feeling that he was meant for something more. He missed Sassy and the freedom of his old life.

One day, Oscar decided he couldn't take it anymore. He packed his bags and said goodbye to Oliver, setting out on the road once again.

As he traveled, Oscar encountered all sorts of challenges. He was chased by dogs and had to dodge passing cars. He was even picked up by a group of traveling circus performers, who tried to turn him into their star attraction.

But Oscar was determined to reach Florida and be with Sassy. He refused to let anything stand in his way.

Finally, after what felt like an eternity, Oscar arrived in Poland. He had made it to the Białowieża Forest, and he knew it was getting dangerous. Bialowieza is the wildest forest in Europe.

As he made his way through the dense forest, Oscar encountered all sorts of dangers. He was chased by a pack of wolves and had to outsmart a group of hunters.

But he also made some unlikely friends, including a deer named Tuna who helped him navigate the forest. Together, they braved the dangers of the wilderness and emerged on the other side.

Oscar knew he still had a long way to go, but he was getting closer to his goal. He was determined to reach Florida and be with Sassy, no matter what it took.

...

After his adventures in the Białowieża Forest, Oscar knew he had one final challenge to overcome: crossing the ocean. He had heard that the best way to get to Florida from Europe was by ship, and he was determined to find a way to get on board.

He scoured the docks, looking for a ship that was heading to Florida. But as he searched, he encountered all sorts of obstacles. Some ships were too crowded, and others had strict no-pets policies.

Just when Oscar was about to give up hope, he stumbled upon a small cargo ship in the port of Douro in Portugal that seemed perfect. The captain was a gruff, no-nonsense man, but Oscar knew he had to take a chance.

He approached the captain and explained his situation. "I need to get to Florida," he said. "Can you help me?"

The captain looked Oscar up and down and let out a deep sigh. "I don't usually allow pets on my ship," he said. "But I have to admit, you're the most determined cat I've ever met. I'll make an exception this time."

Oscar was overjoyed at the captain's words. He knew this was his chance to be with Sassy, and he was willing to do whatever it took to make it happen.

As the ship set sail, Oscar settled into his cabin and tried to get comfortable. But he quickly realized that a member of the ship's crew was allergic to cats, and the journey was not going to be easy.

Every time Oscar ventured out of his cabin, the ship's crew sneezed and sniffled. He grumbled and complained, making it clear that he was not happy to have a feline on board.

But Oscar refused to let the ship's crew's allergies get in the way of his love for Sassy. He found creative ways to stay out of sight and avoid causing the allergic human too much discomfort.

And as the ship sailed across the ocean, Oscar dreamed of the day when he would finally be reunited with Sassy. He knew it would be worth all the challenges he had faced to be by her side.

...

6

After a long and eventful journey, Oscar finally arrived in the United States. He was thrilled to be on American soil, and he knew he was getting closer to Sassy with each passing day.

As he made his way through the bustling streets of New York City, Oscar encountered all sorts of challenges. He had to find food and shelter in a place he knew nothing about, and he had to navigate the unfamiliar city streets.

But he was determined to find Sassy, and he refused to let anything stand in his way. He asked for directions and made friends with the locals, using his charming personality to get by.

As he traveled south toward Florida, Oscar encountered a friendly cat named Sami. Sami was the leader of a group of cat thieves, and he quickly took Oscar under his wing.

"Welcome to the United States, my friend," Sami said. "I can tell you're a cat on a mission. What brings you to our shores?"

Oscar told Sami about his journey to find Sassy, and Sami was touched by his story. He offered to help Oscar find Sassy and offered him a place to stay with the other cat thieves.

Oscar was grateful for Sami's help, and he knew he needed all the friends he could get in a new place like this. He settled into life with the cat thieves and continued his search for Sassy.

As the days passed, Oscar traveled all over Florida, asking anyone he met if they had seen a beautiful white cat named Sassy.

And finally, after what felt like an eternity, he received a tip that led him to Sassy's whereabouts.

He raced to the address he had been given and burst into the house, calling out Sassy's name. And when she appeared in front of him, Oscar knew he had finally found the cat of his dreams.

Sassy was overjoyed to see Oscar, and she threw herself into his arms. They knew they had been through a lot to get to this moment, but they also knew they were meant to be together.

And as they sat together, surrounded by the love and friendship of their new friends, Oscar and Sassy knew they had finally found their happily ever after.

...

Oscar was overjoyed to be reunited with Sassy, and he knew he had finally found the home he had been searching for. He spent his days lounging in the sun and exploring the city with Sassy by his side, and he couldn't believe how lucky he was.

But just when Oscar thought things couldn't get any better, Sassy surprised him with some big news. She had decided to enroll in cat school, and she wanted Oscar to join her.

In Europe, Oscar never heard about anything like cat school. Oscar was skeptical at first. He had never been one for formal education, and he wasn't sure he was cut out for cat school. But Sassy was determined, and she convinced Oscar to give it a try.

As they started their first day of classes, Oscar couldn't help but feel a little out of his depth. He struggled to keep up with the other cats, and he couldn't seem to get the hang of the material.

But Sassy was patient with him, and she encouraged him to keep trying. "You can do this, Oscar," she said. "You just need to focus and apply yourself."

Oscar knew Sassy was right, and he threw himself into his studies. He stayed up late every night, pouring over his textbooks and practicing his skills.

And as the weeks passed, Oscar started to make progress. He found that he actually enjoyed learning, and he started to excel in his classes.

Sassy was proud of Oscar's progress, and she knew he had what it took to succeed. And as they graduated from cat school and set out on the next phase of their lives together, Oscar knew he had Sassy to thank for pushing him to be the best he could be.

...

After their successful stint in cat school, Oscar and Sassy decided to take a break from their studies and embark on a new adventure. They heard about a group of cats who were planning to pull off the biggest cat heist in history, and they knew they had to be a part of it.

The group was led by a clever cat named Shadow, and they were planning to steal a priceless necklace from a wealthy cat's mansion. Oscar and Sassy were excited at the prospect of being part of such a daring mission, and they eagerly joined the team.

As they prepared for the heist, Oscar and Sassy trained hard to hone their skills. They practiced their stealth and agility, and they learned all about the latest cat-burglar technology.

On the night of the heist, Oscar and Sassy were ready. They put on their black cat masks and joined the rest of the team as they snuck into the mansion.

The heist was a success, and Oscar and Sassy made off with the necklace in hand. But just as they were about to make their escape, they were caught by the mansion's security system.

Oscar and Sassy were surrounded by a group of fierce guard cats, and they knew they were in trouble. But they were not about to go down without a fight.

Using all their skills and wits, Oscar and Sassy battled their way out of the mansion and escaped into the night. They were triumphant, and they knew they had pulled off the greatest cat heist in history.

As they returned to their hideout, the other cats hailed them as heroes. Oscar and Sassy were thrilled with their success, and they knew they had made a name for themselves as the top cat thieves in the business.

After their successful heist, Oscar and Sassy became the talk of the cat world. Everyone wanted to know more about the dynamic duo who had pulled off the greatest cat heist in history, and they were suddenly thrust into the spotlight.

Oscar was overwhelmed by the attention, and he wasn't sure how to handle his new-found fame. He was used to living a quiet life in Istanbul, and he wasn't sure he was ready for the limelight.

But Sassy was thrilled with their new celebrity status, and she embraced it with open paws. She loved the attention and the adoration, and she reveled in the opportunity to rub shoulders with the cat elite.

As they navigated their new fame, Oscar and Sassy encountered all sorts of challenges. They were hounded by paparazzi and besieged by fans, and they had to learn how to deal with the constant attention.

But they also enjoyed the perks of their celebrity status. They were invited to all the best parties and events, and they were treated like royalty wherever they went.

Oscar and Sassy had never been happier, and they knew they had each other to thank for it. They had come a long way from their humble beginnings in Istanbul, and they knew they had a bright future ahead of them.

As Oscar and Sassy enjoyed the trappings of their celebrity status, they couldn't help but wonder what the future held. They loved the excitement and adventure of their lives, but they also knew they couldn't live in the fast lane forever.

One day, as they were lounging in the sun, Oscar turned to Sassy and said, "I love our life, but I'm not sure I want to be a cat thief forever. What do you think we should do?"

Sassy thought for a moment and then said, "I've been thinking about that too. I know we love the excitement, but I also want to settle down and have a family someday. Maybe we could use our skills for good instead of just for ourselves."

Oscar was surprised by Sassy's suggestion, but he knew she was right. They had come a long way from their humble beginnings, and they had a lot to be thankful for.

So they decided to use their skills and celebrity status to make a difference in the world. They started a cat rescue organization, and they used their fame to raise awareness and funds for their cause.

As they worked to save cats in need, Oscar and Sassy found a new sense of purpose. They loved the feeling of giving back, and they knew they were making a difference in the world.

And as they settled into their new roles as cat rescuers, Oscar and Sassy knew they had finally found the balance they had been seeking. They had the best of both worlds - the excitement of their old lives and the satisfaction of doing good. It was the perfect combination, and they knew they were meant to be together forever.

When Oscar and Sassy settled into their new roles as cat rescuers, they thought they had finally found the perfect balance in their lives. They loved their work, and they were happy to have a sense of purpose.

But just when they thought they had it all figured out, they were faced with their worst nightmare: Sassy was diagnosed with a serious illness.

Oscar was devastated by the news, and he couldn't bear the thought of losing Sassy. He vowed to do whatever it took to help her get better, and he threw himself into finding a cure.

As they searched for a solution, Oscar and Sassy encountered all sorts of obstacles. They consulted with the best veterinarians and tried every treatment they could think of, but nothing seemed to work.

Oscar was beside himself with worry, and he couldn't help but feel like he was failing Sassy. But Sassy was determined to fight, and she refused to give up.

 As the days passed, Oscar and Sassy remained by each other's side, supporting each other through the hardest times. And finally, after what felt like an eternity, Sassy received some good news: she was going to be okay.

Oscar was overjoyed at the news, and he knew he had Sassy to thank for her strength and perseverance. He vowed to never take a single day with her for granted, and he knew they would face any challenge together as long as they had each other.

…

The Call to Adventure

1

It was a hot and humid summer day in the bustling city of Florida.

Oscar, a scrappy street cat with a love for all things lazy and comfortable, was lounging in the shade of a tree, enjoying a peaceful nap. Suddenly, his peaceful slumber was interrupted by the sound of his cell phone ringing.

"Hello? Who is this?" Oscar grumbled, rubbing his eyes and trying to shake off the sleepiness.

"Oscar, it's Sassy. We have a problem." Sassy's voice came through the phone, sounding urgent and serious.

"Sassy, darling, what's going on?" Oscar asked, sitting up and paying attention.

"There's a group of stray cats who have been captured and are being held against their will. We have to do something about it." Sassy explained, her voice full of determination.

"Oh no, that's terrible. What can we do?" Oscar asked, feeling a sense of urgency.

"We have to rescue them. I'll meet you at our secret base of operations in an hour." Sassy said before hanging up.

Oscar sighed and stood up, stretching his limbs. "Well, I guess my lazy day is over. Time to be a hero." He thought to himself, before setting out on his mission.

As he made his way to the secret base, Oscar encountered all sorts of obstacles and challenges, from dodging busy traffic to avoiding mean dogs. But he was determined to reach his destination and help his fellow felines in need.

Finally, after what seemed like an eternity, Oscar arrived at the secret base, where he was greeted by Sassy, a beautiful and adventurous cat with a sharp wit and a heart of gold.

"Oscar, I'm so glad you made it. We have a lot of work to do." Sassy said, as she handed Oscar a map and a list of supplies they would need for the rescue mission.

"Don't worry, Sassy. I'm always ready for an adventure, especially when it comes to rescuing my fellow cats. And especially when it's with you." Oscar said, winking at Sassy and making her blush.

Together, Oscar and Sassy set out on their mission, determined to save the captured cats and bring the perpetrators to justice. Little did they know, they were in for the adventure of a lifetime.

...

2

Oscar and Sassy spent the next few days gathering as much information as possible about the group of cats who had been captured and the people responsible for their abduction. They scoured the city, talking to other stray cats, prying for clues, and following leads.

"This is harder than I thought. These catnappers are like ghosts, no one seems to know anything about them." Oscar grumbled as they sat on a park bench, trying to make sense of the scattered pieces of information they had collected.

"We can't give up now, Oscar. Those poor cats are counting on us." Sassy said, her voice filled with determination.

"You're right, Sassy. We can't let them down. But how are we going to find out where they're being held?" Oscar asked, scratching his head in frustration.

"I have an idea. Let's go undercover and try to infiltrate the catnapper's network." Sassy suggested, her eyes lighting up with excitement.

"Undercover? Sassy, are you sure that's a good idea? What if we get caught?" Oscar asked, feeling a sudden surge of anxiety.

"Don't worry, Oscar. I have a plan. Trust me." Sassy said, patting Oscar's paw reassuringly.

And so, Oscar and Sassy set out on their undercover mission, determined to gather as much information as possible and bring the catnappers to justice. They dressed up in disguises and went undercover, pretending to be interested in buying cats from the catnappers. It was a risky mission, but they were determined to succeed.

After several days of investigation, they had gathered enough evidence to bring the catnappers to justice. But as they were making their way back to their secret base, they were caught by the catnappers and barely managed to escape with their lives.

"Sassy, that was a close call. I don't know if I can handle any more undercover missions like that." Oscar said, panting and out of breath as they made their way back to the secret base.

"Don't worry, Oscar. We're almost there. We just need to come up with a plan to rescue the captured cats and bring down the entire trafficking operation." Sassy said, her voice full of determination.

Oscar sighed and nodded, determined to see the mission through to the end. Together, he and Sassy would stop at nothing to save the captured cats and bring the catnappers to justice.

...

3

After much discussion and planning, Oscar and Sassy decided that the best way to rescue the captured cats and bring down the entire trafficking operation was to infiltrate the catnapper's compound and gather as much evidence as possible. It was a risky plan, but they were determined to succeed.

"Are you sure this is a good idea, Sassy? What if we get caught?" Oscar asked as they approached the compound in the dead of night.

"Don't worry, Oscar. I have a plan. Just follow my lead and everything will be fine." Sassy said, her voice full of confidence.

Oscar nodded, trying to steady his nerves. He followed Sassy as she snuck into the compound, using all of her stealth and cunning to avoid detection.

As they made their way through the compound, they were confronted by the catnapper's henchmen, a group of tough and menacing cats. But Sassy was quick on her feet and managed to distract them, allowing Oscar to slip past and gather the evidence they needed.

After several tense and adrenaline-filled minutes, Oscar and Sassy had gathered all of the evidence they needed and made their way back to the secret base, triumphant and relieved.

"Sassy, that was amazing. You were like a ninja out there." Oscar said as they sat in the safety of the secret base, going over the evidence they had collected.

"Thanks, Oscar. But we're not out of the woods yet. We still have to analyze this evidence and come up with a plan to rescue the captured cats and bring down the entire operation." Sassy said, her voice serious.

Oscar nodded, feeling a renewed sense of determination. Together, he and Sassy would stop at nothing to rescue the captured cats and bring the catnappers to justice.

...

4

After gathering all of the evidence from their infiltration of the catnapper's compound, Oscar and Sassy set to work analyzing it and trying to make sense of it all.

"This is a lot of information to go through, Sassy. I hope we can find something useful." Oscar said as they sifted through the piles of documents and recordings.

"Don't worry, Oscar. We'll find something. We just have to be persistent." Sassy said, her eyes narrowed in concentration.

As they worked, they began to realize that the catnappers were part of a larger network of animal traffickers, operating not just in Florida but all across the country. It was a sobering realization, but it also gave them a new sense of purpose.

"Sassy, we can't let these traffickers get away with this. We have to bring them down." Oscar said, his voice filled with determination.

"I agree, Oscar. We have to gather more information and come up with a plan to take down the entire operation." Sassy said, nodding in agreement.

And so, Oscar and Sassy set out to gather more information and come up with a plan to bring down the entire trafficking operation. It was a difficult and dangerous mission, but they were determined to succeed. They worked tirelessly, piecing together clues and following leads, determined to put an end to the catnappers' nefarious activities once and for all.

As they worked, they also found time to enjoy their relationship, sharing funny jokes and romantic moments as they took breaks from their mission. It was a challenging and exhilarating time, but they were in it together, determined to see it through to the end.

...

5

With their plan in place, Oscar and Sassy decided that the best way to gather more information and bring down the entire trafficking operation was to go undercover once again. It was a risky plan, but they were determined to succeed.

"Sassy, are you sure this is a good idea? What if we get caught again?" Oscar asked as they prepared to set out on their mission.

"Don't worry, Oscar. We have a solid plan and we're better prepared this time. Trust me." Sassy said, patting Oscar's paw reassuringly.

Oscar sighed and nodded, trusting in Sassy's instincts and determination. Together, they set out on their undercover mission, determined to gather as much information as possible and bring the traffickers to justice.

As they worked, they encountered all sorts of obstacles and challenges, from dodging suspicious glances to avoiding detection. But they were determined to succeed, and they used all of their wit and cunning to outsmart their foes and gather the information they needed.

Finally, after several days of intense and adrenaline-filled undercover work, Oscar and Sassy had gathered all of the information they needed to bring down the entire trafficking operation. They made their way back to the secret base, triumphant and relieved.

"Sassy, we did it! We have all of the information we need to bring down the entire operation." Oscar said as they sat in the safety of the secret base, going over the evidence they had collected.

"I couldn't have done it without you, Oscar. You were amazing out there." Sassy said, leaning in to give Oscar a hug.

Oscar smiled and hugged Sassy back, feeling grateful for their friendship and the adventures they had shared together. They were one step closer to rescuing the captured cats and bringing the traffickers to justice, and they were determined to see it through to the end.

...

6

With all of the information they needed to bring down the entire trafficking operation, Oscar and Sassy set to work on the final step of their plan: rescuing the captured cats and bringing the traffickers to justice.

"Sassy, what do you think is the best way to rescue the cats and bring down the traffickers?" Oscar asked as they sat in the secret base, going over their options.

"I think we should go in guns blazing," Sassy said, her eyes lighting up with excitement.

"Guns blazing? Sassy, we're cats. We don't have guns." Oscar pointed out, raising an eyebrow.

"Oh, right. Well, then we'll just have to use our wits and cunning instead." Sassy said, grinning mischievously.

Oscar nodded, feeling a surge of determination. Together, they would stop at nothing to rescue the captured cats and bring the traffickers to justice.

As they worked on their rescue plan, they encountered all sorts of obstacles and challenges, from scouting out the location of the captured cats to avoiding detection. But they were determined to succeed, and they used all of their wit and cunning to outsmart their foes and rescue the cats.

Finally, the day of the rescue arrived. Oscar and Sassy put their plan into action, sneaking into the compound and rescuing the captured cats. It was a tense and dramatic mission, but they were determined to succeed.

As they made their escape, they were pursued by the traffickers, who were determined to stop them at any cost. But Oscar and Sassy were one step ahead, using all of their skills and resourcefulness to outmaneuver their foes and make their way to safety.

...

7

With the captured cats safely in their paws, Oscar and Sassy set out on their great escape, determined to bring the traffickers to justice and put an end to their nefarious activities once and for all.

"Sassy, how are we going to get out of here? The traffickers are hot on our tail!" Oscar shouted as they ran through the streets and alleys of the city, trying to shake off their pursuers.

"Don't worry, Oscar. I have a plan. Follow me!" Sassy shouted, leading the way through a series of tight twists and turns.

Oscar followed Sassy, his heart racing as they darted through the city, avoiding detection and outmaneuvering their pursuers at every turn. It was a high-speed chase that tested their skills and resourcefulness to the limit.

As they made their escape, they encountered all sorts of obstacles and challenges, from dodging busy traffic to avoiding mean dogs. But they were determined to succeed, and they used all of their wit and cunning to outsmart their foes and make their way to safety.

Finally, after what seemed like an eternity, Oscar and Sassy emerged victorious, panting and out of breath but safe and sound.

"Sassy, we did it!

With the captured cats safe and the traffickers hot on their heels, Oscar and Sassy knew that they had to act fast in order to bring the traffickers to justice and put an end to their nefarious activities.

"Sassy, we have to go to the authorities and report what we've learned. We can't let these traffickers get away with this." Oscar said, his voice filled with determination.

"I agree, Oscar. But we have to be careful. The traffickers are dangerous and they'll stop at nothing to silence us." Sassy said, her eyes narrowed in determination.

Oscar nodded, his mind racing as he tried to come up with a plan. Finally, he had an idea.

"I have an idea. We can go to the authorities and report what we've learned, but we'll do it anonymously. That way, we can stay safe and still bring the traffickers to justice." Oscar said, his voice full of excitement.

"That's a great idea, Oscar. We'll do it. But we have to be careful. These traffickers are dangerous and they'll stop at nothing to silence us." Sassy said, nodding in agreement.

And so, Oscar and Sassy set out on their mission, determined to bring the traffickers to justice and put an end to their nefarious activities.

They went to the authorities and reported what they had learned, taking care to remain anonymous and avoid detection.

It was a risky and dangerous mission, but they were determined to succeed. And in the end, their efforts paid off, as the authorities were able to arrest the traffickers and put an end to their criminal activities.

Oscar and Sassy were hailed as heroes, their bravery and determination inspiring cats all across the city. And as they stood together, looking out at the city they had helped to protect, they knew that they had made a difference and that they would always be there for each other, through thick and thin.

...

8

"Sassy, can you believe it? We did it! We brought down the entire trafficking operation and saved all of those poor cats." Oscar said, his eyes shining with pride.

"I couldn't have done it without you, Oscar. You were amazing out there." Sassy said, leaning in to give Oscar a hug.

Oscar blushed and hugged Sassy back, feeling grateful for their friendship and the adventures they had shared together.

But as they basked in the glow of their success, they knew that the work wasn't over yet. There were still other traffickers out there, preying on innocent animals and causing suffering and misery.

"Sassy, we can't let this happen again. We have to do something to stop these traffickers once and for all." Oscar said, his voice filled with determination.

"I agree, Oscar. We have to spread the word and educate other cats about the dangers of animal trafficking. We have to do everything we can to put an end to this terrible practice." Sassy said, nodding in agreement.

And so, Oscar and Sassy set out on a new mission, determined to spread the word and educate other cats about the dangers of animal trafficking. They traveled all across the city, sharing their story and their knowledge, determined to make a difference and bring about lasting change.

As they traveled and worked together, they also found time to enjoy their relationship, sharing funny jokes and romantic moments as they took breaks from their mission. It was a challenging and exhilarating time, but they were in it together.

...

9

As Oscar and Sassy traveled the city, spreading the word about animal trafficking and educating other cats about the dangers of this terrible practice, they also took time to enjoy the great outdoors and all of the adventures it had to offer.

"Sassy, look at this beautiful park! We have to explore it." Oscar said, his eyes shining with excitement as they approached a sprawling green space filled with trees, flowers, and a babbling stream.

"Oh, Oscar, it looks amazing. But we have to be careful. There could be all sorts of dangers lurking in the great outdoors." Sassy said, her eyes narrowed in caution.

Oscar nodded, taking Sassy's words to heart. Together, they set out to explore the park, using all of their wit and cunning to navigate its many dangers and enjoy all of its wonders.

As they roamed the park, they encountered all sorts of obstacles and challenges, from dodging busy squirrels to avoiding mean birds. But they were determined to have fun and enjoy the great outdoors, and they used all of their skills and resourcefulness to overcome these challenges and make the most of their adventure.

Finally, Oscar and Sassy emerged from the park, panting and out of breath but exhilarated and full of joy.

"Sassy, that was amazing! I can't wait to explore more of the great outdoors with you." Oscar said, his eyes shining with excitement.

"I can't wait either, Oscar. The great outdoors is full of wonders and adventures, and I'm so glad we can experience them together." Sassy said, leaning in to give Oscar a hug.

Oscar smiled and hugged Sassy back, feeling grateful for their love and the adventures they had shared together.

...

Solve the Mystery

1

It was a typical lazy afternoon for Oscar and Sassy. Oscar was sprawled out on the porch, basking in the sun and enjoying a delicious bowl of tuna. Sassy was curled up next to him, purring contentedly.

"Ahh, this is the life," Oscar sighed, patting his belly. "No work, no stress, just lounging around all day. I love being a street cat."

Sassy chuckled. "You certainly have a knack for the art of relaxation, Oscar. But sometimes I think you could use a little more excitement in your life."

Oscar snorted. "Excitement? No thank you. I'll stick to my cozy little routine, thank you very much."

Just then, they heard a loud crash from a nearby house. Oscar and Sassy sat up, alert and curious.

"What was that?" Oscar said, peering towards the house.

"I don't know, but I have a feeling our cozy little routine is about to be disrupted," Sassy said, jumping to her feet. "Come on, let's investigate!"

Oscar groaned but reluctantly followed Sassy as she scampered towards the house. They crept up to a window and peered inside. To their shock, they saw a shadowy figure rummaging through the homeowner's belongings.

"Whoa, we've got a thief on our paws!" Oscar exclaimed.

"We have to do something!" Sassy said, her eyes flashing with determination. "We can't let this criminal get away with it!"

Oscar's eyes widened. "Wait, hold on. We're just two ordinary cats. How are we supposed to stop a thief?"

Sassy grinned. "Oh, I have a feeling we'll find a way. Maybe we can do some detective work and gather some clues. Or we could use our feline charm and seduce the thief into giving themselves up."

Oscar rolled his eyes. "Uh, I think we'll stick with the detective work. But first, we have to figure out how to get into this house without getting caught."

As they tried to come up with a plan, they were startled by a loud meowing. They turned to see a group of cats approaching, all of them wearing detective hats and carrying magnifying glasses.

"Ahoy there, fellow felines!" one of the cats called out. "We heard about your predicament and decided to lend a paw. Allow us to introduce ourselves: we are the Furry Detective Agency!"

Oscar and Sassy couldn't help but laugh at the sight of the comical group of cats. "Uh, thanks for the offer," Oscar said. "But we think we can handle this on our own."

"Suit yourself," the leader of the group said, shrugging. "But if you need any help, don't hesitate to give us a call. We're always ready for a good mystery."

With that, the Furry Detective Agency waved goodbye and scampered off, leaving Oscar and Sassy to their own devices.

"Well, that was certainly an obstacle I didn't see coming," Oscar said, shaking his head.

"Come on, let's get back to work," Sassy said, grinning. "We've got a thief to catch!"

And with that, Oscar and Sassy set off on their adventure, determined to bring the thief to justice and restore peace to their neighborhood.

...

Oscar and Sassy crept up to the window and peered inside, trying to get a better look at the thief. To their surprise, they saw that the thief was actually a small, scrappy-looking kitten with a mask over its face.

"A kitten thief?" Oscar whispered, raising an eyebrow. "Well, that's a first."

"Don't let their size fool you," Sassy whispered back. "They could still be dangerous."

The kitten seemed to be talking to themselves, muttering about a valuable item they were searching for. Oscar and Sassy exchanged a glance, realizing that this could be their chance to gather some clues.

"I have an idea," Oscar said, his eyes lighting up. "We'll follow the thief and see where they go. Maybe we can find out more about this valuable item they're after."

Sassy nodded. "Good plan. But we have to be careful. We don't want them to catch us."

The kitten finished rummaging through the house and started to make its way towards the door. Oscar and Sassy darted out of sight, waiting for the thief to leave before following them.

They tailed the kitten through the streets, trying to stay out of sight. The kitten seemed to be in a hurry, darting through alleys and jumping over fences. Oscar and Sassy struggled to keep up, panting and stumbling in their pursuit.

"This is harder than it looks," Oscar panted. "I think I'm getting a cramp."

"Come on, Oscar, you can do it!" Sassy encouraged him. "We can't let this kitten get away."

Just as they were about to lose sight of the thief, they turned a corner and came face to face with a pack of snarling dogs. The kitten froze, looking terrified.

"Oh no, we're doomed!" Oscar exclaimed, his eyes wide with fear.

Sassy quickly sprang into action, hissing and scratching at the dogs. "Get back, you mangy mutts! Leave us alone!"

The dogs backed off, yipping and barking in surprise. The kitten seized the opportunity and made a run for it, disappearing into the shadows.

"Whew, that was a close one," Oscar said, wiping his brow. "Thanks for saving us, Sassy."

Sassy shrugged. "No problem. But we have to be more careful. We can't let our guard down for a second."

As they continued their pursuit, Oscar couldn't help but feel a sense of excitement and adventure. He had never done anything like this before, and he was starting to see the appeal of a little excitement in his life again.

"You know, Sassy, I have to admit, this is kind of fun," he said, grinning. "I never thought I'd enjoy chasing after a thief, but here I am, loving every minute of it."

Sassy chuckled. "I told you, Oscar. A little excitement can be a good thing. And who knows, maybe we'll even catch our thief and solve the mystery."

"I hope so," Oscar said, his eyes sparkling with determination. "Because I'm not ready to give up on this adventure just yet."

...

3

Oscar and Sassy were hot on the tail of the kitten thief, determined to catch them and uncover the mystery of the valuable item they were searching for. However, they were in for a surprise when the thief turned and caught sight of them.

"Uh oh, we've been spotted!" Oscar exclaimed, his eyes wide with alarm.

"Don't panic, just keep running!" Sassy called out, darting through the streets.

The kitten thief let out a yowl of anger and chased after them, snarling and baring their teeth. Oscar and Sassy ran as fast as they could, their hearts pounding with fear and excitement.

"This isn't exactly how I imagined this real adventure going," Oscar panted, his legs aching with the effort. "I thought there would be more lounging and less running for my life."

"Well, that's the price of fame, I guess," Sassy teased, her eyes sparkling with amusement. "But I have a feeling things are only going to get more interesting from here on out."

As they fled through the streets, they were chased by the kitten thief and a growing number of barking dogs. They turned corners and darted through alleys, trying to shake off their pursuers. Just when they thought they were safe, they found themselves backed into a dead end.

"Oh no, we're trapped!" Oscar cried out, his eyes scanning the area for an escape route.

Sassy narrowed her eyes, a determined look on her face. "We're not going down without a fight. Let's show these dogs who's boss!"

As the dogs closed in, Oscar and Sassy stood their ground, hissing and scratching at their attackers. They fought with all their might, using their quick reflexes and cunning to outsmart the dogs.

Just when they thought they were done for, they heard a loud yowling and a group of cats appeared, leaping into the fray and helping Oscar and Sassy fend off the dogs.

"We've got your back, fellow felines!" one of the cats called out, her eyes blazing with determination. "We won't let these mangy mutts hurt you!"

Oscar and Sassy couldn't help but laugh at the sight of the comical group of cats, dressed in detective hats and wielding magnifying glasses. They were the Furry Detective Agency, the group of cats they had met earlier.

"Well, I'll be," Oscar said, grinning. "Looks like we have some unexpected allies."

"Glad to see you guys again," Sassy said, grinning back. "We could use all the help we can get."

Together, Oscar, Sassy, and the Furry Detective Agency fought off the dogs and chased the kitten thief away. As the dust settled, they all let out a sigh of relief.

"Well, that was certainly an adventure," Oscar said, panting and covered in dirt and scratches. "I don't think I've ever run that much in my life."

"You did great, Oscar," Sassy said, nuzzling him affectionately. "I'm so proud of you for stepping out of your comfort zone and helping me solve this mystery."

Oscar blushed, feeling a warm glow of pride. "Well, I couldn't have done it without you, Sassy. You were amazing out there. You really know how to take charge and kick butt."

Sassy chuckled. "Thanks, Oscar. But we still have a long way to go. We still don't know what that valuable item is that the thief was after, and we don't have any leads on where they could be hiding."

Oscar nodded. "Right. We have to keep searching and gathering clues. Maybe we can ask around and see if anyone knows anything about the thief or the item."

They set off through the streets, questioning other cats and trying to gather information. However, they hit a dead end at every turn, and they were starting to get frustrated.

"This is harder than I thought it would be," Oscar said, sighing in defeat. "We don't seem to be getting anywhere."

Sassy patted his shoulder. "Don't worry, Oscar. We'll figure it out. We just have to keep trying."

Just as they were about to give up, they heard a faint meowing in the distance. They turned to see a small, scrappy-looking kitten walking towards them, its tail dragging on the ground.

"Hello there, little guy," Sassy said, approaching the kitten with a friendly smile. "Do you know something about the thief we're looking for?"

The kitten looked up at them with big, sad eyes. "Yes, I do. I know where they're hiding."

Oscar and Sassy's eyes lit up. "Really? That's exactly what we've been looking for! Can you take us to them?"

The kitten nodded. "Yes, but it's not going to be easy. They're hiding in a place that's very hard to get to. You'll have to be brave and careful."

Oscar and Sassy exchanged a glance, their hearts racing with excitement. "We're ready for the challenge," Oscar said, his eyes blazing with determination. "Take us to the thief!"

The kitten led them through the streets and into a dark, abandoned warehouse. As they crept through the shadows, they were confronted by a group of menacing-looking cats, all of them armed and dangerous.

"Looks like we've found the thief's hideout," Sassy whispered, her eyes narrowing. "We have to be careful. These cats won't go down easily."

Oscar nodded, his heart pounding with fear and excitement. "Right. Let's do this."

Together, they charged into the warehouse, fighting off the thief's accomplices and chasing the kitten thief through the maze of corridors. It was a wild and intense battle, but Oscar and Sassy were determined to catch the thief and bring them to justice.

Finally, they cornered the kitten thief in a room.

...

4

Oscar and Sassy stood face to face with the kitten thief, their hearts racing with excitement and adrenaline. The thief snarled at them, their eyes filled with hatred and fear.

"Give up, thief," Sassy said, her voice calm and steady. "You're surrounded and outnumbered. It's over."

The thief let out a yowl of rage and made a break for it, darting past Oscar and Sassy and disappearing into the shadows. Oscar and Sassy exchanged a glance, then took off after the thief.

"Come back here, you little criminal!" Oscar shouted, his voice echoing through the warehouse.

They chased the thief through the corridors, their paws pounding against the ground as they raced after their prey. The thief was fast, but Oscar and Sassy were determined to catch them.

As they turned a corner, they were confronted by a group of cats blocking their path. The cats were all dressed in black, with menacing scowls on their faces.

"Uh oh, this doesn't look good," Oscar said, his eyes wide with alarm.

Sassy narrowed her eyes, a determined look on her face. "We're not backing down. We've come too far to give up now."

The cats charged at Oscar and Sassy, snarling and hissing. Oscar and Sassy fought back with all their might, using their quick reflexes and cunning to outsmart their opponents. It was a fierce and intense battle, but they were determined to catch the thief and bring them to justice.

Finally, after what felt like an eternity, the thief stumbled and fell to the ground, panting and exhausted. Oscar and Sassy approached them, their eyes blazing with determination.

"It's over, thief," Sassy said, her voice firm and steady. "You're coming with us."

The thief let out a sob, their shoulders shaking with tears. "Please, don't turn me in. I didn't mean to steal. I was just trying to get by.

...

5

Oscar and Sassy stood over the defeated kitten thief, their hearts racing with excitement and relief. The thief looked up at them with big, sad eyes, their shoulders shaking with tears.

"Please, don't turn me in," the thief begged, their voice small and pleading. "I didn't mean to steal. I was just trying to get by."

Oscar and Sassy exchanged a glance, their hearts melting at the sight of the little kitten. They had been so focused on catching the thief and solving the mystery, they hadn't stopped to consider the thief's motivations.

"Why were you trying to steal?" Sassy asked, her voice soft and gentle.

The thief sniffled, their eyes filling with tears. "I was orphaned when I was just a baby. I've been on my own ever since, trying to survive on the streets. I was desperate, and I thought maybe if I had something valuable, I could trade it for a place to stay or some food."

Oscar and Sassy's hearts went out to the kitten. They couldn't imagine what it must be like to be alone and struggling on the streets.

"We won't turn you in," Sassy said, her voice firm but kind. "But you can't go on stealing. It's not right. There are other ways to get by."

The thief nodded, their eyes filling with gratitude. "Thank you. I'll do whatever it takes to make things right. I just want a place to belong and someone to care for me."

Oscar and Sassy looked at each other, their hearts overflowing with love and compassion. They knew exactly what the kitten needed.

"We'll take you in," Oscar said, his voice soft and gentle. "You can come and live with us. We'll make sure you have a warm bed and all the food you can eat. And most importantly, you'll have a family who loves you."

The kitten's eyes lit up, and they threw their arms around Oscar and Sassy, sobbing with gratitude. "Thank you, thank you! I promise I'll be the best cat I can be. I'll never steal again."

Oscar and Sassy hugged the kitten back, their hearts overflowing with love and joy. They had caught the thief, but they had also gained a new family member.

…

6

Oscar and Sassy were feeling pretty pleased with themselves. They had caught the kitten thief, solved the mystery, and even gained a new family member in the process. Life was good.

"Well, that was certainly an adventure," Oscar said, stretching out on the couch and letting out a contented sigh. "I don't think I've ever run that much in my life. My paws are killing me."

Sassy chuckled and curled up next to him. "It was worth it, though. We caught the thief and helped out a little kitten in need. That's what being a detective is all about."

Oscar nodded, a warm glow of pride filling his chest. "Yeah, you're right. It feels good to do something good for the world."

Just then, there was a knock at the door. Oscar and Sassy exchanged a glance, then got up to answer it. When they opened the door, they were confronted by a group of cats dressed in detective hats and carrying magnifying glasses.

"We're the Furry Detective Agency," the leader of the group said, his voice serious and stern. "We've heard about your recent case and we want to offer you a job."

Oscar and Sassy looked at each other, their eyes wide with surprise. "A job?" they said in unison.

"Yes," the leader said, a sly smile crossing his face. "We've heard about your skills and we think you'd make excellent additions to our team. What do you say?"

Oscar and Sassy looked at each other, their hearts racing with excitement. They had always dreamed of being real detectives, and now they had the opportunity.

"We'll take it!" they said in unison, grinning from ear to ear.

The leader of the Furry Detective Agency smiled and shook their paws. "Welcome aboard. We have a lot of work to do, but I have a feeling we're going to make an excellent team."

Oscar and Sassy couldn't help but laugh at the comical group of cats, all of them dressed in detective gear and wielding magnifying glasses. They were the Furry Detective Agency, and they were ready to take on the world.

"Bring on the mysteries!" Oscar said, his eyes sparkling with excitement. "We're ready for anything!"

Sassy chuckled and leaned in for a kiss. "As long as we're together, we can handle anything the world throws at us."

Oscar and Sassy grinned at each other, their hearts overflowing with love and adventure.

...

Meeting the Pharaoh's Cat

1

Oscar the laziest cat sat on his favorite spot on the couch, lazily grooming his fur as he watched the world go by outside his window. Sassy, his beloved feline companion, sat next to him, twirling a strand of yarn between her paws.

"Oscar, have you ever thought about traveling?" Sassy asked, her bright green eyes sparkling with excitement. "I've always wanted to see the pyramids in Egypt. Imagine all the adventures we could have!"

Oscar let out a leisurely yawn, his pink tongue lolling out of his mouth. "Meh, I'm content just lounging around here. The idea of all that walking and exploring sounds exhausting."

Sassy rolled her eyes and gave him a playful swat with her paw. "Come on, Oscar, where's your sense of adventure? We could see so many new things and meet all kinds of interesting cats. Plus, think of all the delicious treats we could try!"

Oscar's stomach rumbled at the mention of treats, and he gave Sassy a thoughtful look. "Well, I do love trying new foods... and I suppose it would be nice to see some new places. But what about all the obstacles we might face on our journey? What if we get lost or run into danger?"

Sassy chuckled and nuzzled Oscar's cheek. "Don't worry, my love. We'll face any challenges together. And think of all the romance and drama we could have on our journey! It will be an adventure to remember."

Oscar couldn't deny that the prospect of spending time with Sassy, exploring new places, and having grand adventures was tempting. He let out a sigh and stood up, stretching his sleek black fur.

"All right, Sassy. You've convinced me. Let's go to Egypt and see the pyramids. And maybe eat some tasty treats along the way."

Sassy purred and nuzzled him again, her eyes shining with love and excitement. "Oh, Oscar, I knew you had it in you! This is going to be the best adventure ever!"

And with that, the laziest cat and his adventurous feline companion set off on their journey to Egypt, ready for all the drama, romance, and excitement that lay ahead.

...

<h1 style="text-align:center">2</h1>

Oscar and Sassy packed their bags and set off on their journey to Egypt, filled with excitement and a sense of adventure. As they traveled, they encountered all kinds of challenges and obstacles.

At one point, they found themselves lost in a bustling city, with no idea how to get to the airport. "Great, just great," Oscar grumbled, his whiskers twitching with frustration. "We've been wandering around for hours, and we still have no idea where we're going."

Sassy gave him a reassuring nuzzle and grinned. "Don't worry, Oscar. We'll find our way eventually. And think of all the funny stories we'll have to tell when we get home."

As they wandered through the crowded streets, they encountered all kinds of interesting characters, including a street performer who juggled flaming torches and a group of friendly kittens who offered to help them find their way.

Despite the challenges they faced, Oscar and Sassy remained determined and optimistic, finding humor and romance in even the most difficult situations.

Finally, they arrived at the airport and boarded their plane, ready to begin the next leg of their journey. It was convenient for them to travel in a plane as a new rule was imposed by the international cat rights organization (ICO) for all airlines. So they flew over the vast expanse of the desert, Oscar couldn't help but feel a sense of awe and excitement at the thought of all the adventures that lay ahead.

"Sassy, can you believe it? We're really going to Egypt!" he exclaimed, his green eyes sparkling with excitement.

Sassy purred and nuzzled his cheek. "Yes, my love. And I can't wait to see all the amazing sights and have all sorts of romantic and dramatic adventures with you."

And with that, the two cats settled in for the long flight, ready to take on whatever challenges and obstacles lay ahead in their quest to see the pyramids and explore all that Egypt had to offer.

...

3

Oscar and Sassy arrived in Egypt, their senses overwhelmed by the sights, sounds, and smells of the bustling city of Cairo. They made their way to the pyramids, marveling at the towering structures as they approached.

"Wow, they're even more impressive up close!" Oscar exclaimed, his eyes wide with wonder.

Sassy nodded, her tail twitching with excitement. "I know, right? And just think of all the history and mystery that's hidden within these walls. I can't wait to explore and see what secrets we can uncover!"

As they began to explore the pyramids, they encountered all sorts of obstacles and challenges. They had to navigate through narrow corridors and climb steep staircases, all while avoiding traps and avoiding the attention of guards.

"Ugh, I can't believe I let you talk me into this," Oscar grumbled, huffing and puffing as he climbed a particularly steep staircase. "My paws are killing me, and I'm pretty sure I have a crick in my tail."

Sassy chuckled and gave him a playful nudge. "Oh, stop complaining. Think of all the amazing sights we're seeing and the amazing stories we'll have to tell when we get home. And besides, the romance and drama will be worth it in the end."

Despite the challenges they faced, Oscar and Sassy persevered, determined to uncover all the secrets the pyramids had to offer. And as they explored deeper into the ancient structures, they discovered all sorts of hidden chambers and mysterious artifacts, their sense of wonder and excitement growing with each new discovery.

...

4

As Oscar and Sassy explored the pyramids, they stumbled upon a hidden chamber filled with ancient artifacts and treasures. In the center of the room sat a regal-looking cat with golden fur and piercing green eyes.

"Greetings, travelers," the cat said, his voice deep and commanding. "I am the Pharaoh's personal cat, and I have been entrusted with the power to transport those worthy enough through time."

Oscar and Sassy stared at the cat in amazement, their mouths hanging open. "Time travel? That's impossible!" Oscar exclaimed.

The Pharaoh's cat chuckled and gave them a sly wink. "Oh, but it is possible, my friends. And I believe that you two have the courage and determination to make the journey. Are you ready to see the wonders of ancient Egypt for yourselves?"

Sassy's eyes lit up with excitement, and she gave Oscar a pleading look. "Oh, Oscar, please say yes! This is the opportunity of a lifetime!"

Oscar hesitated, his paws twitching with nervousness. Time travel was a daunting prospect, and he wasn't sure he was ready for such a grand adventure. But as he looked into Sassy's hopeful eyes, he knew he couldn't let her down.

"All right, I'm in," he said, his voice shaking slightly. "But if we get stuck in the past and can't get back, I'm blaming you."

The Pharaoh's cat chuckled and gestured for them to follow him. "Fear not, my friends. The journey will be filled with adventure, drama, and romance. And I have no doubt that you will return home safe and sound."

And with that, Oscar and Sassy embarked on their journey through time, ready to experience the wonders of ancient Egypt and all the obstacles and challenges that lay ahead.

...

5

As Oscar and Sassy followed the Pharaoh's cat through the hidden chamber, they felt a strange sensation wash over them. Suddenly, the world around them began to blur and swirl, and they found themselves transported back in time to ancient Egypt.

"Whoa, what just happened?" Oscar exclaimed, his eyes wide with wonder and confusion.

The Pharaoh's cat chuckled and gave them a knowing smile. "Welcome to ancient Egypt, my friends. The power of time travel is a mysterious and wondrous thing."

As they explored the ancient city, Oscar and Sassy encountered all sorts of fascinating characters and learned about the culture and customs of the time. They met temple priests, who told them about the gods and goddesses worshipped in ancient Egypt and learned about the intricate hieroglyphics that adorned the walls of the temples.

They also had to navigate all sorts of challenges and obstacles, such as dodging the stampeding hooves of a herd of wild donkeys and outwitting a group of thieving street urchins.

Despite the challenges they faced, Oscar and Sassy remained determined and adventurous, their love and bond growing stronger with each new adventure they shared.

"Oscar, this has been the most amazing adventure ever," Sassy said, snuggling close to him as they watched the sunset over the pyramids. "I'm so glad we came on this journey together."

Oscar nuzzled her cheek and purred. "Me too, Sassy. And I can't wait to see what other adventures and obstacles we'll face on our journey through time."

As the night fell, Oscar and Sassy settled down to rest, ready to tackle whatever challenges the next day might bring.

...

6

As Oscar and Sassy explored ancient Egypt, they stumbled upon a mystery that needed to be solved. It seemed that a valuable artifact had been stolen from one of the temples, and the priests were beside themselves with worry.

"Oh, this is terrible!" one of the priests exclaimed, wringing his hands. "The artifact is a sacred and powerful symbol of the goddess Isis. Without it, the temple will lose its power and prestige."

Oscar and Sassy knew they had to help solve the mystery and recover the artifact. "Don't worry, we'll help you find it," Sassy said, her eyes determined.

"Yeah, we're pretty good at solving mysteries and outwitting thieves," Oscar added, puffing out his chest.

As they set out to solve the mystery, they encountered all sorts of obstacles and challenges. They had to sneak past guards and avoid detection, all while trying to gather clues and gather information.

Despite the difficulties they faced, Oscar and Sassy remained determined and worked together as a team, using their quick wit and clever thinking to outsmart the thieves and recover the artifact.

"We did it!" Sassy exclaimed, holding up the artifact triumphantly. "We solved the mystery and recovered the artifact!"

Oscar let out a triumphant meow and nuzzled Sassy's cheek. "We make a great team, Sassy. And I'm so glad we could help the priests and restore the temple's power and prestige."

As they returned the artifact to the grateful priests and received their thanks and blessings, Oscar and Sassy knew that their journey through ancient Egypt had been a truly memorable and amazing adventure.

...

7

After solving the mystery and recovering the artifact, Oscar and Sassy knew it was time to return home to the present day. As they prepared to make the journey back through time, they couldn't help but feel a sense of sadness at leaving behind the amazing adventures and experiences they had had in ancient Egypt.

"I can't believe our journey is coming to an end," Sassy said, her green eyes misty with emotion. "I've loved every moment of our adventure, and I'll never forget all the amazing sights and experiences we've had."

Oscar nuzzled her cheek and purred. "Me neither, Sassy. But I'm excited to see what other adventures and obstacles we'll face in the future. And besides, we can always come back and visit ancient Egypt anytime we want."

As they made their way back to the hidden chamber and prepared to make the journey through time, they encountered all sorts of challenges and obstacles. They had to avoid being caught by the guards and evade a group of bandits who were determined to steal their treasure.

Despite the dangers they faced, Oscar and Sassy remained determined and stuck together, their bond and love for each other stronger than ever.

Finally, they emerged from the hidden chamber and found themselves back in the present day.

"We made it!" Oscar exclaimed, his green eyes shining with joy. "We're home!"

Sassy nuzzled him and purred. "Yes, we are. And I can't wait to see what other amazing adventures and obstacles we'll face in the future."

As they set off on the next leg of their journey, Oscar and Sassy knew that no matter what challenges and obstacles lay ahead, they would always face them together, their love and bond stronger than ever.

...

8

After their amazing journey through ancient Egypt, Oscar and Sassy were excited to return home to Florida and share their stories and adventures with their friends and loved ones.

As they flew back to the US, Oscar couldn't help but feel a sense of excitement and anticipation. "I can't wait to see all our friends and tell them about our adventures in Egypt," he said, his green eyes sparkling with excitement.

Sassy chuckled and nuzzled his cheek. "I know me too. And I can't wait to see our little kitten, Billy. He's probably grown so much since we left."

As they landed in Florida and made their way back to their home, they were greeted with open arms by their friends and loved ones. Billy, the kitten they had adopted on their journey, ran up to them and tackled them with a flurry of purrs and licks.

"Oscar! Sassy! You're back!" he exclaimed, his eyes shining with joy.

Oscar chuckled and nuzzled Billy's cheek. "Yes, we are. And we have so many amazing stories to tell you about our journey to Egypt and all the obstacles and adventures we faced."

As they settled back into their home and began to share their stories with their friends and loved ones, Oscar and Sassy couldn't help but feel grateful for the amazing adventure they had had and the love and bond they shared.

"I'm so glad we decided to go on this journey together, Sassy," Oscar said, snuggling close to her as they watched the sunset over the ocean.

Sassy purred and nuzzled his cheek. "Me too, Oscar. And I can't wait to see what other amazing adventures and obstacles we'll face in the future."

As they cuddled up together and watched the sunset, Oscar and Sassy knew that no matter what challenges and obstacles lay ahead, they would always face them together, their love and bond stronger than ever.

The Epilogue

1

Oscar and Sassy sat on the windowsill of their cozy Florida home, gazing out at the bright sunshine and palm trees. It had been several years since Oscar had left Istanbul and embarked on his new life in the United States with his love.

"Do you ever miss Istanbul, Oscar?" Sassy asked, turning to her beloved companion.

Oscar sighed and stretched out his paws. "Of course I do, Sassy. It's where we first met, after all. But I'm happy here with you. We have a good life."

Sassy nodded, her tail twitching. "I know. But sometimes I just can't shake the feeling that you left something important behind in Istanbul. You know it?"

Oscar nodded, understanding exactly what Sassy meant. Oscar had his old lazy lives behind in Istanbul, and though they had made a new home for themselves in Florida, there was always a sense of longing for the past.

"Maybe we should go back," Oscar said suddenly, surprising even himself with the suggestion.

Sassy's eyes widened. "Really? You want to go back to Istanbul?"

Oscar nodded. "I think it's time. We've been here long enough, and I miss the food, the culture, the sights and sounds of the city. And most of all, I miss our old friends and the adventures we used to have."

Sassy hesitated, her tail twitching nervously. "But what about our life here? Our home, our friends, our routine?"

Oscar reached out and nuzzled her affectionately. "We can always come back to visit, Sassy. And who knows, maybe we'll find new adventures and make new memories in Istanbul."

Sassy considered this for a moment, then nodded. "Okay, Oscar. Let's do it. Let's go back to Istanbul."

And with that, Oscar and Sassy packed their bags and set off on a new adventure, leaving behind the comfort and familiarity of their Florida home and embarking on a journey back to the city they had left behind.

As they traveled, Oscar and Sassy encountered many obstacles and challenges, from language barriers and cultural differences to unexpected delays and mishaps. But through it all, they remained determined and optimistic, relying on their wit, bravery, and most of all, their love for each other to see them through.

And as they finally arrived back in Istanbul, they knew that no matter what challenges lay ahead, they would face them together, united by the strong bond of friendship and love that had brought them back to the city they called home.

...

2

As Oscar and Sassy wandered through the winding streets of Istanbul, taking in the sights, sounds, and smells of the city they had missed so much, they couldn't help but feel a sense of excitement and nostalgia.

"Look, Oscar, there's the old market where we used to sneak bites of fish from the vendors," Sassy said, pointing to a bustling open-air market in the distance.

Oscar chuckled. "And there's the park where we used to chase each other around in circles for hours."

As they walked, they were stopped by a group of cats they had known in their previous life in Istanbul.

"Oscar! Sassy! Is it really you?" one of the cats, a sleek Siamese named Luna, exclaimed in disbelief.

Oscar and Sassy nodded, grinning from ear to ear. "It's us, Luna," Sassy said, giving her old friend a hug.

The group of cats chatted and caught up, reminiscing about old times and filling each other in on all the changes and happenings in their lives since they had last seen each other.

"Oh, you have to meet my new mate, Max," Luna said, pulling a handsome orange tabby towards the group. "He's just moved to Istanbul from London."

As they all caught up and made new friends, Oscar and Sassy couldn't help but feel grateful for the warm welcome they had received back in Istanbul. Despite the challenges and obstacles they had faced on their journey, they knew that they were right where they belonged, surrounded by the friends and community they had left behind.

But as the sun began to set and the group began to say their goodbyes, Oscar and Sassy couldn't shake a sense of unease. They had left behind a comfortable life in Florida and returned to Istanbul with the hope of rekindling old memories and making new ones, but as they said their goodbyes and parted ways with their old friends, they couldn't help but wonder what the future held for them in this new chapter of their lives.

...

3

As Oscar and Sassy settled into their new life in Istanbul, they couldn't help but feel a sense of longing for the family they had left behind in Florida. Despite the joy of being reunited with old friends and the excitement of starting a new chapter in their lives, something was missing.

One day, as they were out exploring the city, they stumbled upon a small kitten huddled in an alleyway, shivering and alone. Without hesitation, Oscar and Sassy scooped up the kitten and brought her home, determined to give her the love and care she deserved.

"What should we name her?" Sassy asked as the kitten snuggled up to her.

Oscar thought for a moment. "How about Lucky? She's lucky we found her, and we're lucky to have her as part of our family."

Sassy nodded, smiling. "Lucky it is. Welcome to the family, Lucky."

As they cared for Lucky and watched her grow, Oscar and Sassy began to feel a sense of joy and purpose they had been missing. Lucky brought to light and laughter into their lives, and they were grateful to have her by their side.

But despite the happiness, Lucky brought, Oscar and Sassy couldn't shake the feeling that something was off. They had left behind a comfortable life in Florida and returned to Istanbul with the hope of rekindling old memories and making new ones, but they couldn't help but wonder if they had made a mistake.

As they struggled with their doubts and fears, they leaned on each other and on their beloved Lucky, finding comfort and strength in their bond and the love they shared. And as they faced the challenges and obstacles that lay ahead, they knew that as long as they were together, they could overcome anything.

...

4

As Oscar and Sassy settled into their new life in Istanbul, they couldn't help but feel a sense of unease. Despite the joy of being reunited with old friends and the happiness of raising Lucky, they couldn't shake the feeling that something was off.

One day, as they were out exploring the city, they stumbled upon a group of cats huddled in a corner, looking frightened and distressed.

"What's going on?" Sassy asked, approaching the group cautiously.

"It's that man," one of the cats, a scruffy calico named Whiskers, said, his voice shaking. "He hates animals, and he's been causing trouble for us all."

Oscar and Sassy exchanged a worried look. They had heard stories of humans who hated animals, and they knew that such people could be dangerous and cruel.

"What can we do?" Sassy asked, determined to help the other cats.

"We don't know," Whiskers said, shaking his head. "We've tried to stay out of his way, but he always seems to find us. We're terrified of what he might do."

Oscar and Sassy knew they had to do something. They couldn't stand by and let this man harm the innocent cats of Istanbul.

"We'll help you," Oscar said firmly, his tail twitching with determination. "We'll do whatever it takes to stop this man and keep you all safe."

As they made a plan and prepared to take action, Oscar and Sassy couldn't help but feel a sense of fear and uncertainty. They had faced many challenges and obstacles in their lives, but this was different. This was a fight for something greater than themselves, and they knew that the stakes were high.

But as they stood together, united in their determination to protect the cats of Istanbul, Oscar and Sassy knew that they were ready for whatever came their way. They would do whatever it took to keep their loved ones safe, even if it meant putting their own lives on the line.

...

5

Oscar and Sassy stood on the rooftops of Istanbul, gazing out at the city spread out before them. They had spent the past few days gathering information and making a plan to stop the man who hated animals and was causing trouble for the city's cats.

"Are you ready, Sassy?" Oscar asked, turning to his beloved companion.

Sassy nodded, her eyes shining with determination. "I'm ready, Oscar. Let's do this."

Together, they set off on their mission, using all their skills and bravery to track down the man and put an end to his reign of terror. They fought off his minions and battled their way through countless obstacles, never giving up and always putting the safety of the other cats first.

Finally, after what seemed like an eternity, they reached the man himself. He was a towering figure, with a cruel sneer and a heart full of hatred. But Oscar and Sassy were not afraid. They stood their ground, determined to put an end to his reign of terror once and for all.

In a fierce and epic battle, Oscar and Sassy fought with all their might, using their agility and quick thinking to outmaneuver the man and finally defeat him. As they stood victorious, the other cats cheered and celebrated, grateful to be free of the man's tyranny.

Oscar and Sassy were hailed as heroes, celebrated by the cats of Istanbul as the ones who had saved them from the man who hated animals. They basked in the glory and adoration, but deep down, they knew that it was their love for each other and for the other cats that had truly driven them to succeed.

As they returned home, tired but triumphant, Oscar and Sassy knew that they had made a difference and that they had cemented their place as heroes in the hearts of the cats of Istanbul.

...

6

Oscar and Sassy were sitting on the windowsill of their Istanbul home, enjoying the warm sunshine and each other's company. It had been a year since they had returned to the city and faced the man who hated animals, and they had settled into a comfortable routine, filled with love, adventure, and purpose.

But as they sat together, basking in the warmth of the sun, a sense of unease washed over Oscar. He couldn't shake the feeling that something was off, that something was coming that would change their lives forever.

One day, Oscar sat on the windowsill of his Istanbul home, staring out at the city as the sun set behind the skyline. As he sat there, lost in thought, a knock at the door startled him. He stood up, his heart racing as he made his way to the door.

As he opened it, he was met with the grave faces of his old friends, Luna, and Whiskers.

"What is it?" Oscar asked, his voice shaking.

Luna's eyes were filled with tears as she spoke. "It's Sassy. She's been in an accident. Someone killed her. She's... she's gone."

Oscar felt his world shatter as the words sank in. Sassy, his beloved companion, the love of his life, was gone.

As he fell to the ground, overwhelmed with grief, Oscar knew that he would never be the same. Sassy had been his everything, and without her, he didn't know how he could go on.

As the tears flowed freely down his face, Luna and Whiskers tried to console him, but their words seemed hollow and empty. Oscar knew that nothing could fill the hole in his heart left by Sassy's loss.

As the days passed, Oscar's grief turned to anger and outrage. He couldn't understand how anyone could do something so cruel and heartless, and he vowed to find the person responsible and make them pay for their actions.

Through his connections in the cat community, Oscar was able to track down the man who had killed Sassy. He was a known animal hater, with a long history of cruelty and abuse towards cats and other animals.

Oscar's friends and family tried to talk him out of seeking revenge, but he was consumed by a burning desire for justice. He knew that he couldn't bring Sassy back, but he could at least make sure that the man who had taken her from him paid for his actions.

As he planned his revenge, Oscar couldn't shake the feeling that he was making a mistake. He knew that violence and hatred would only lead to more pain and suffering, and he didn't want to become the kind of cat he despised.

But as he thought about Sassy and the love they had shared, he knew that he couldn't let her death go unpunished. He had to do something, no matter the cost.

So, with a heavy heart and a fierce determination, Oscar set out to confront the man who had taken everything from him.

He followed him through the city, staying hidden in the shadows as he watched him go about his day. As he stalked him, he couldn't help but feel a sense of disgust and revulsion at the sight of him.

Finally, when the man was alone and vulnerable, Oscar made his move. He attacked him with all the strength and ferocity he could muster, clawing and biting until the man lay defeated and bleeding at his paws.

As he stood over him, panting and covered in blood, Oscar realized that he had made a terrible mistake. He had let his anger and hatred consume him, and he had become the very thing he had despised.

He looked down at the man he had attacked, Oscar was filled with a sense of shame and regret. He had let his grief and anger lead him down a path of violence and hatred, and he knew that he had to turn back before it was too late.

As he turned to leave, he was confronted by a group of cats who had witnessed the attack. They looked at him with disgust and disappointment, and Oscar knew that he had let them all down.

...

Oscar sat alone in his Istanbul home, surrounded by silence and emptiness. Sassy, the love of his life, was gone, and he didn't know how to go on.

Days passed, and Oscar barely moved from his spot on the windowsill. He refused to eat or drink, lost in a fog of grief and despair. Lucky, the kitten they had taken in, tried her best to cheer him up, but nothing seemed to reach him.

As the weeks went by, Oscar's friends and family grew worried. They had never seen him like this, and they feared for his health and well-being.

"Oscar, please, you have to eat something," Luna pleaded, offering him a bowl of his favorite food.

Oscar shook his head, his eyes empty and distant. "I can't, Luna. I can't do anything without Sassy. She was my everything."

Luna's heart ached as she watched her friend suffer. She knew that Oscar needed time to grieve, but she also knew that he couldn't stay stuck in this dark place forever.

The days dragged on, and Luna and the other cats tried everything they could think of to help Oscar out of his grief. They took him on walks, played games with him, and even tried to set him up on a date with a charming calico named Ginger.

But nothing seemed to work. Oscar remained lost in his grief, barely able to function or find any joy in life.

As the months passed, Oscar's friends and family began to lose hope. They had never seen anyone grieve like this, and they feared that Oscar would never be able to move on.

But just when all seemed lost, a glimmer of hope appeared on the horizon.

...

8

Oscar sat on the windowsill, staring out at the Istanbul skyline as the sun set behind the city. He had been lost in grief for months, unable to find any joy or purpose in life since the loss of Sassy.

But as he sat there, something shifted inside him. He couldn't quite put his paw on it, but he felt a glimmer of hope, a spark of something he hadn't felt in a long time.

As he sat there, lost in thought, Lucky approached him, her tail wagging with excitement.

"Oscar, come on, let's go out and explore the city," she said, tugging on his paw.

Oscar hesitated, then stood up and followed Lucky out the door. As they wandered the streets of Istanbul, he couldn't help but feel a sense of nostalgia and longing for the adventures he and Sassy had shared in this city.

But as he walked, he also felt a sense of possibility and hope. He had been stuck in his grief for so long, but now, he realized that he had a choice. He could stay stuck in the past, or he could embrace the present and find a way to move on.

As he walked, Oscar began to feel a sense of healing and acceptance. He would never forget Sassy or the love they had shared, but he knew that he had to find a way to live his life without her.

With Lucky by his side, Oscar began to explore the city, rediscovering all the joys and wonders it had to offer. He reconnected with old friends, made new ones, and even started a new hobby, painting beautiful landscapes of the city.

When he rediscovered his passions and found a sense of purpose, Oscar began to heal. He would always carry the pain of Sassy's loss with him, but he also knew that he had the strength and resilience to move on and create a new life for himself, filled with love, adventure, and hope.

...

9

Oscar stood at the airport, gazing out at the planes taking off and landing as he waited for his flight to Florida. It had been several years since he had left Istanbul and returned to the place where he and Sassy had first fallen in love.

When he waited, he couldn't help but feel a mix of emotions. On one hand, he was excited to see his old friends and family and to visit the places that held so many memories for him and Sassy. On the other hand, he was filled with a sense of sadness and loss, knowing that he would never be able to share these experiences with the love of his life.

The plane began to take off, Oscar knew that he had to see this through. He didn't want to live in the city that took his love for his wonderful life. He had to return to Florida, to face the past and the memories that lingered there. He had to find a way to let go and move on, once and for all.

As the plane flew through the clouds, Oscar couldn't help but feel a sense of nostalgia and longing for the life he had left behind. But he also knew that he had to face the future with courage and hope and find a way to honor the love he had shared with Sassy, even as he moved on and built a new life for himself.